ALL ABOARD THE GOODNIGHT TRAIN

Words by STEPHANIE CALMENSON
Music by FRANK METIS (ASCAP)

arr. by Frank Metis

Copyright © 1984 Grosset & Dunlap, Inc.

For my father

Text copyright © 1984 by Stephanie Calmenson.
Illustrations copyright © 1984 by Normand Chartier.
All rights reserved. Published by Grosset & Dunlap,
a division of The Putnam Publishing Group, New York.
Published simultaneously in Canada.
Printed in the United States of America. ISBN: 0-448-11226-4.
Library of Congress Catalog Card Number: 84-080664.

ALL ABOARD THE GOODNIGHT TRAIN

Written by Stephanie Calmenson
Illustrated by Normand L. Chartier

Publishers • GROSSET & DUNLAP • New York

Contents

Can I Stay Up?   **7**

Star Light, Star Bright   **17**

Jungle Lullaby   **26**

All Aboard the Goodnight Train   **37**

Can I Stay Up?

"I'm not ready to go to sleep yet," Brown Bear said to his mother and father. "Can I stay up to watch *The Mr. Rabbit Show?* Can I, please?"

"It's been a long day," said Mrs. Bear. "You were up early for school, and you played with Moose all afternoon."

"Get ready for bed now," said Mr. Bear. "Then we'll see about TV."

Brown Bear put on his bumblebee pajamas, washed his face, and brushed his teeth. All these bedtime chores were making Brown Bear sleepy. He rested his head on the sink and dropped off to slcep.

"Brown Bear!" he heard his mother call. "Do you need some help?"

Brown Bear opened his eyes quickly. For a minute he thought it was morning. Then he remembered it was nighttime, and soon *The Mr. Rabbit Show* would be on.

"I'm almost ready," Brown Bear answered.

"I'd like to let you stay up," said Mr. Bear, "but you look awfully sleepy to me."

"I'm not sleepy!" said Brown Bear. "Watch!"

Brown Bear jumped up and down ten times in a row.

"You see, a sleepy bear could not do that."

"OK," said Mr. Bear. "Run and get your blanket, so you'll be nice and warm."

Brown Bear ran to his room and came back
with his blanket, his pillow, and Barney, too.
"I promised Barney he could watch the
show, since he was such a good bear all day."

Brown Bear snuggled down under the blanket, fluffed up the pillow for his head, and hugged Barney close to his side.

Mr. Bear turned on the TV. *The Mr. Rabbit Show* was just going on.

To start, Mr. Rabbit told rabbit riddles. Brown Bear knew every answer. Mr. Rabbit sang a song. Brown Bear knew all the words. Then Mr. Rabbit introduced his first guests.

"Would you please welcome The
Woodland Ballet Company in a dance from
The Sleeping Beauty?"

"Oh, I like that!" said Brown Bear, sitting
up tall. "In school I was the Prince."

He watched happily as the Princess leaped
and twirled across the stage.

Then suddenly there came a clash of cymbals, and the Princess was put under a spell. She was to sleep for one hundred years.

"I will have to wake her," said Brown Bear.

But Brown Bear started feeling a little sleepy himself. As a gentle harp began to play, the Lilac Fairy appeared, waving her magic wand.

"Ahhh," sighed Brown Bear. "This music...is making me...so..."

Brown Bear closed his eyes, and soon Mr.
Bear carried his sleeping prince to bed.

Star Light, Star Bright

"Come, my little elephant! It's your bathtime," Elephant's mother called.

"But, Mommy, my play is tomorrow. I have to practice," said Elephant.

"Say your part once more now," said Elephant's mother. "Then it will be time to rest."

Elephant began:

> *Oh, who is so merry, so merry,*
> *heigh ho!*
> *As the light-hearted fairy?*
> *heigh ho, heigh ho!*
> *She dances and sings,*
> *To the sound of her wings,*
> *With a hey and a heigh and a ho!*

"Bravo!" cried Elephant's father.

"And now," said Elephant's mother, "with a hey and a heigh and a ho, it's into the bath we go!"

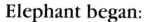

"Do you really think I will be good in the play tomorrow?" asked Elephant.

"You will be just fine," said Elephant's mother. "And if you make a little mistake, that's OK, too. Now please hurry into the tub, so we can get you to bed."

19

As soon as Elephant had been tucked in, she
began to worry.

"What if I forget my lines? What if no one
can hear me?" Then she had an idea. "I'll
make a wish on a star."

But when Elephant looked out her window,
she couldn't find a star. She began to cry.

Her mother came into the room. "What is
making my little elephant so sad?"

Elephant stopped crying long enough to tell her.

"I was going to wish on a star that everyone would hear me and that I wouldn't forget my lines. But I can't find a star!"

"The star is there," said Elephant's mother. "It's just covered by clouds. You make your wish. The star will hear you."

"I wanted to *see* the star," said Elephant.

Elephant's mother went right to work with tin foil and string. It wasn't long before she went back to Elephant's room.

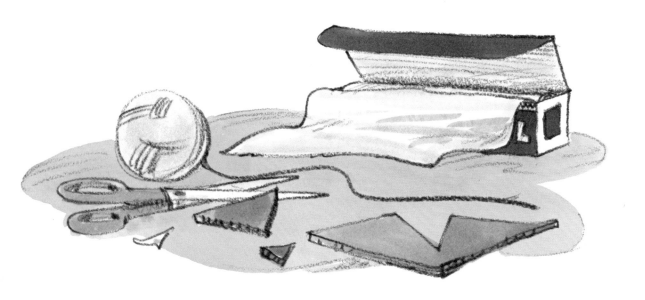

Elephant was sitting up in bed with a worried look on her face.

"Here is your own special wishing star," said Elephant's mother.

She hung up the star and kissed Elephant goodnight.

Star light, star bright,
First star I see tonight.
Wish I may, wish I might,
Have the wish, I wish tonight.

Elephant made her wish and fell fast asleep,
knowing that tomorrow everything would be
all right.

And it was.

Jungle Lullaby

Monkey was staying with his Grandma and Grandpa. It was his first night away from home.

He and Grandpa were finishing their puzzle when the telephone rang.

Grandma went to answer it, then called, "Monkey! It's for you!"

Monkey picked up the phone.

"Hello, Mommy! Hello, Daddy! Yes, I'm having a very good time. No, I didn't know it was bedtime."

Monkey listened as his mommy and daddy wished him goodnight.

"I love you, too," said Monkey. "See you in the morning!"

"OK, young fellow," said Grandpa. "It's time to go to sleep."

While Monkey was getting ready for bed, he thought about his mother and father. He was happy to be at Grandma and Grandpa's house, but he would miss his goodnight kisses and his song.

"Would you like to hear a story?" Grandma and Grandpa asked.

"No, thank you," said Monkey.

"If there is anything you need, just call us," Grandpa said. "Sleep well. We love you."

Monkey closed his eyes, but he couldn't sleep. "Grand-pa!" he called.

Grandpa came into the room and asked, "What would you like, Monkey?"

"Can I have a drink of water?"

"Of course," said Grandpa.

When Grandpa came back with the glass of water, Monkey took only a sip.

"Thank you," he said.

Grandpa kissed him goodnight and turned out the light.

Again, Monkey closed his eyes but couldn't sleep. "Grand-pa!" he called.

"Did you forget something, Monkey?"

"I need to go the bathroom," Monkey said.

Grandpa took Monkey to the bathroom and waited until he was done. Then he tucked Monkey in.

Monkey closed his eyes but still couldn't sleep. He waited as long as he could, then gave a loud *ah-choo!* and called, "Grand-pa!"

Grandpa came in carrying a box of tissues. "Did I hear you sneeze, Monkey?"

"Yes, Grandpa," said Monkey. He took a tissue from the box and patted his nose.

33

"Is there something bothering you?" asked
Grandpa.

"I miss Mommy and Daddy," Monkey said.
"They always sing me a song before I go to
sleep."

"We sang lots of songs to your daddy when
he was just your size," said Grandpa. "The one
he liked best was 'Jungle Lullaby'."

"That's it! That's the song they sing to me!"
cried Monkey.

"I'm not sure I remember the words," said Grandpa.

"I know them!" Monkey said.

> *In the jungle lives a monkey,*
> *Who goes swinging through the trees.*
> *He eats bananas when he's hungry,*
> *And he chatters in the breeze.*
> *When he's sleepy he climbs higher,*
> *Makes a cradle in the leaves.*
> *Where his mama gently sways him,*
> *Says, goodnight, and have sweet dreams.*

When Monkey finished, he saw that
Grandpa was sleeping. He put his arms around
him and went to sleep, too.

All Aboard the Goodnight Train

Duck had invited her friends Pig, Lamb, and Goat to her house for a pajama party.

"Let's play school," said Duck. "I'll be the teacher."

"You were Teacher last time," said Pig. "I want to be Teacher."

"No, *me*!" shouted Lamb and Goat together.

Mrs. Duck came into the room.

"It's getting too noisy in here," she said. "I want you to have a good time, but you must be quieter."

"We can't decide who'll be Teacher," said Duck.

"Why don't you pick straws?" suggested Mrs. Duck.

Mrs. Duck took a cup of straws from the shelf. They each picked one.

"I got Number 1!" said Lamb. "So I'm the teacher first. Who would like to draw?" she asked.

"Me! Me! Me!" called Duck, Pig, and Goat.

"A little less noise, please," said Lamb. "Duck, would you be our monitor today?"

39

Duck handed out paper and crayons, and everyone began to draw. Even the teacher.

"Can I have the red crayon, Duck?" asked Pig. "I'm drawing an apple."

"Can't it be a yellow apple?" asked Duck. "I need the red crayon."

"You've had it a long time," Pig said, her voice growing louder. "It's my turn!"

Lamb decided it was time for the teacher to help.

"Is there another part of your picture you can color, Duck? I see you have the ocean on your paper, too."

"Yes, Teacher," said Duck. "But now I'll need *your* crayon!"

Goat thought this was very funny.

"Share your crayon, Teacher," she said, laughing.

Lamb quickly colored the rest of her sky blue. "Ding! Ding!" she said. "School is over. Goodbye!"

41

"Let's play train," said Goat. "Who wants to go to the moon?"

"Rocket ships go to the moon, not trains," said Pig. "We need a conductor. The conductor will know where this train is going."

Just then, Mrs. Duck walked in.

"Here's the conductor!" said Duck.

"Can you tell us where this train is going?" asked Pig.

"It's bedtime," said Mrs. Duck, "so the next stop will be Sleepytown. All aboard The Goodnight Train!" she called.

"Toot! Toot!" sang out the four friends as they scrambled under the covers.

When everyone had settled down,
Mrs. Duck quietly began:

> *The Goodnight Train is here now,*
> *It's right at your front door.*
> *So gather dreams and wishes,*
> *That's what this train is for.*
> *Have your ticket ready,*
> *One warm kiss goodnight.*
> *Then all aboard The Goodnight Train,*
> *Sleep safe till morning light.*

They each gave Mrs. Duck a ticket—
one warm kiss goodnight. Then they
closed their eyes and went to sleep.

JUNGLE LULLABY

Words by **STEPHANIE CALMENSON**
Music by **FRANK METIS (ASCAP)**

arr. by Frank Metis